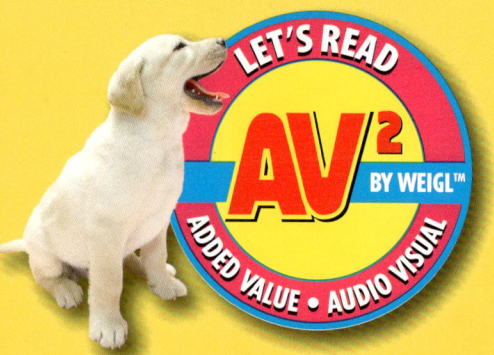

AV² provides enriched content that supplements and complements this book. Weigl's AV² books strive to create inspired learning and engage young minds in a total learning experience.

Your AV² Media Enhanced books come alive with...

 **Audio** Listen to sections of the book read aloud.

 **Key Words** Study vocabulary, and complete a matching word activity.

 **Video** Watch informative video clips.

 **Quizzes** Test your knowledge.

 **Embedded Weblinks** Gain additional information for research.

 **Slide Show** View images and captions, and prepare a presentation.

 **Try This!** Complete activities and hands-on experiments.

...and much, much more!

Go to www.av2books.com, and enter this book's unique code.

BOOK CODE

G793444

AV² by Weigl brings you media enhanced books that support active learning.

Published by AV² by Weigl
350 5th Avenue, 59th Floor New York, NY 10118
Website: www.av2books.com

Copyright ©2016 AV² by Weigl
All rights reserved. No part of this publication may be reproduced, stored in a retrieval system, or transmitted in any form or by any means, electronic, mechanical, photocopying, recording, or otherwise, without the prior written permission of the publisher.

Library of Congress Control Number: 2015937782

ISBN 978-1-4896-3621-8 (hardcover)
ISBN 978-1-4896-3622-5 (softcover)
ISBN 978-1-4896-3623-2 (single user eBook)
ISBN 978-1-4896-3624-9 (multi-user eBook)

Printed in the United States of America in Brainerd, Minnesota
1 2 3 4 5 6 7 8 9 0 19 18 17 16 15

072015
070715

Editor: Katie Gillespie   Design and Layout: Ana María Vidal

Every reasonable effort has been made to trace ownership and to obtain permission to reprint copyright material. The publisher would be pleased to have any errors or omissions brought to its attention so that they may be corrected in subsequent printings.

Weigl acknowledges Getty Images and iStock as the primary image suppliers for this title.

Let's Celebrate American Holidays

Halloween

CONTENTS

- 2 AV² Book Code
- 4 When Is Halloween?
- 6 What Is Halloween?
- 8 Trick-or-Treating
- 10 Halloween Costumes
- 12 Coming Together
- 14 How We Celebrate
- 16 More Traditions
- 18 Helping Others
- 20 Special Celebrations
- 22 Halloween Facts
- 24 Key Words/Log on to www.av2books.com

Halloween is celebrated on October 31st every year. It began as a day to mark the start of the winter season.

Over time, the holiday became a fun day for children to dress up in costumes and eat sweet treats.

Halloween began thousands of years ago as a festival called Samhain. It was a holiday celebrated by Celtic people in ancient Britain and Ireland.

Samhain is an old Irish word that means "summer's end."

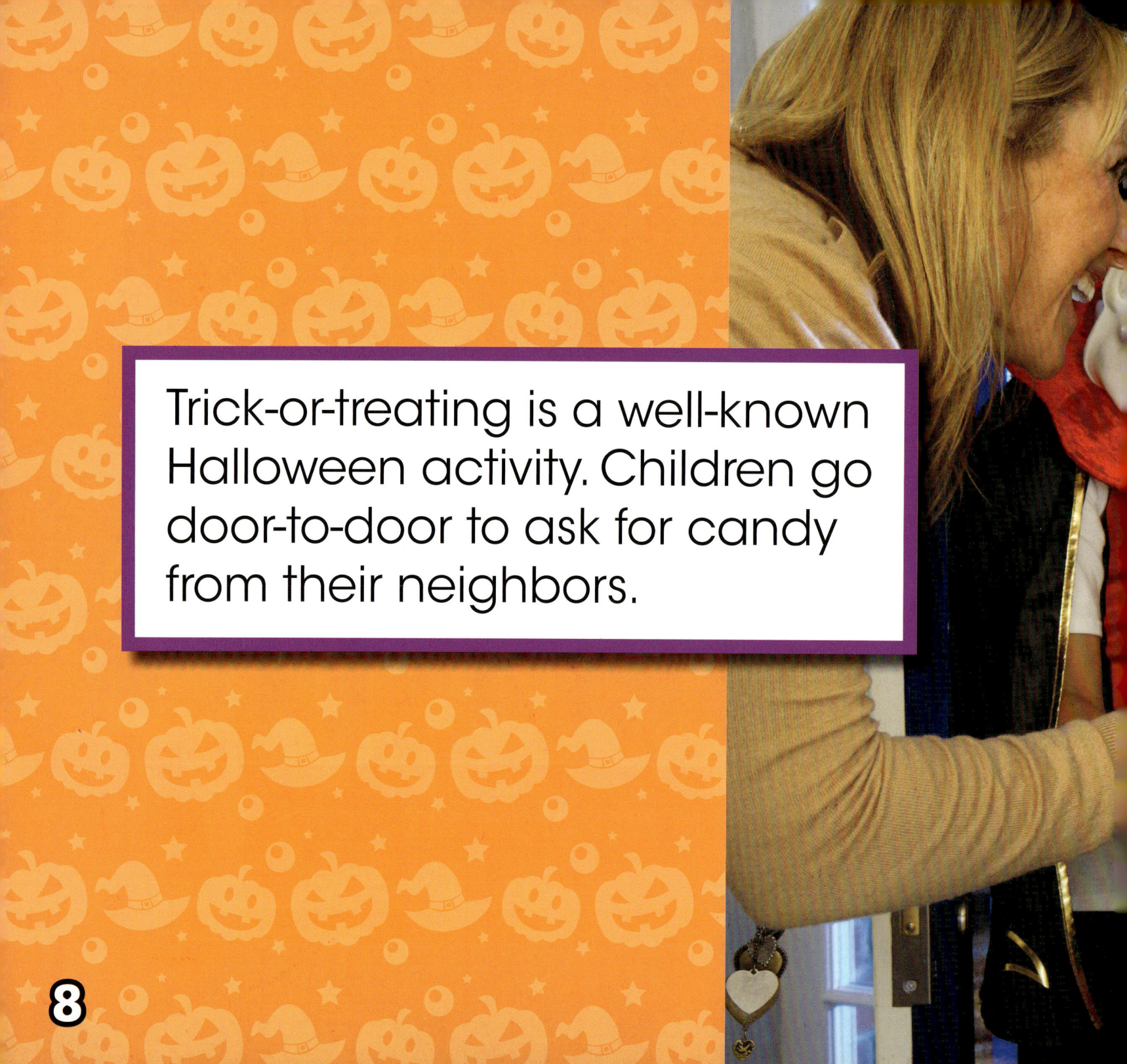

Trick-or-treating is a well-known Halloween activity. Children go door-to-door to ask for candy from their neighbors.

People often wear costumes on Halloween. Spooky monsters such as vampires or zombies are popular choices.

Some people throw parties to celebrate Halloween. Often, treats are served, and festive games are played.

Bobbing for apples is a fun Halloween party game.

Today, candy is the best-known Halloween food. Many people hand out chocolate bars or other sweets to trick-or-treaters.

Apples are a more traditional Halloween food.

15

Many people decorate their homes for Halloween. Fake skeletons, tombstones, and spider webs are often used.

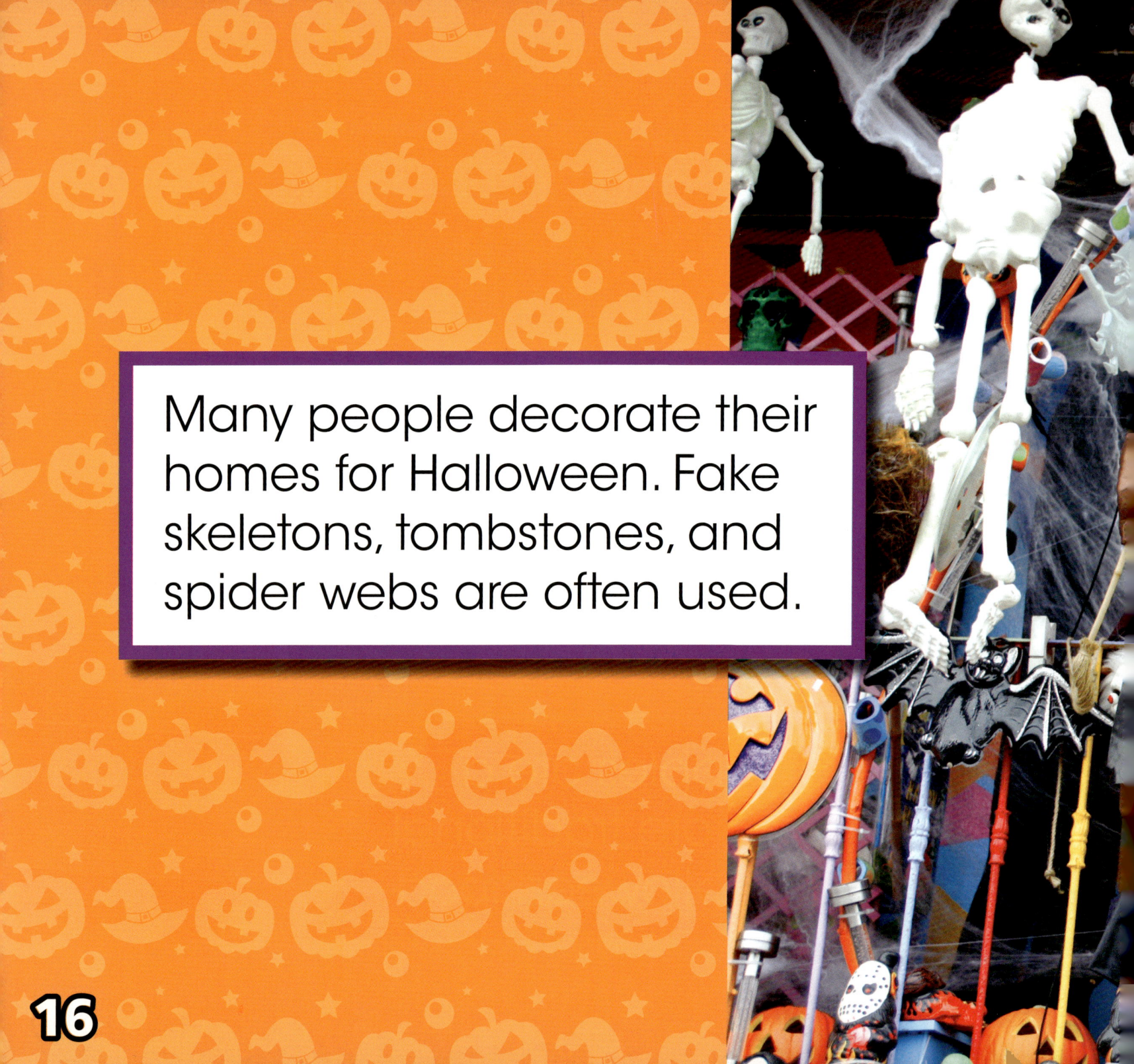

Halloween is a time to help others. Children across America collect money for the Trick-or-Treat for UNICEF program.

UNICEF stands for the United Nations Children's Fund.

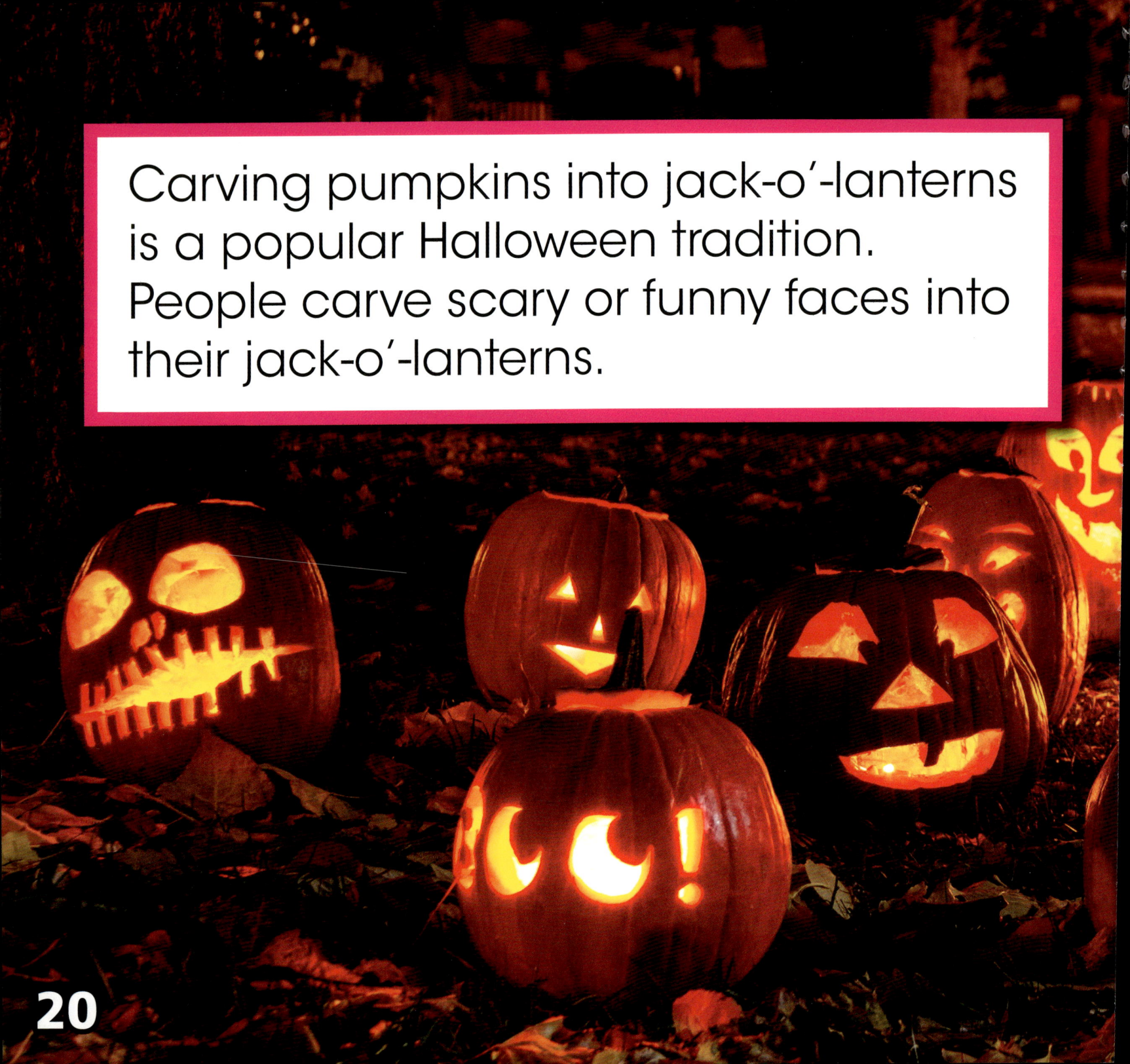

Carving pumpkins into jack-o'-lanterns is a popular Halloween tradition. People carve scary or funny faces into their jack-o'-lanterns.

Some of the first jack-o'-lanterns were made out of turnips.

HALLOWEEN FACTS

These pages provide more detail about the interesting facts found in the book. They are intended to be used by adults as a learning support to help young readers round out their knowledge of each holiday featured in the *Let's Celebrate American Holidays* series.

Pages 4–5

Halloween is celebrated on October 31st every year. The holiday originally took place at the end of harvest time, when crops were ripe. Today, Halloween is celebrated in many different countries around the world. It has become a very popular holiday in the United States. In some places, such as Mexico and South America, Halloween celebrations continue until November 2nd.

Pages 6–7

Halloween began thousands of years ago as a festival called Samhain. Some well-known Halloween symbols, such as black cats and bats, date back to this festival. The term *Halloween* comes from a Christian holiday that took place around the same time as Samhain. November 1st, or All Saints' Day, is a day to honor the saints of the Christian church. This was called "All Hallows" in medieval England. The night before, "All Hallows Eve," was shortened to Halloween over time.

Pages 8–9

Trick-or-treating is a well-known Halloween activity. It originates from an old Irish tradition. All Soul's Day is a Christian holiday that falls on November 2nd every year. It is a day to pray for the souls of people who have passed away. On the day before All Soul's Day, the poor would travel from house to house asking for food in exchange for prayers for lost loved ones. Special pastries known as "soul cakes" were given in return for these prayers.

Pages 10–11

People often wear costumes on Halloween. The tradition of wearing costumes dates back to the festival of Samhain. People thought that the souls of the dead wandered around during this time, along with creatures, such as witches and fairies. Over time, people began dressing as these beings. People still wear costumes today, from scary werewolves to brave superheroes and beautiful princesses. Contests are often held, with prizes awarded for the best costumes.

22

Pages 12–13  **Some people throw parties to celebrate Halloween.** A traditional Halloween party game, bobbing for apples, may have medieval roots. Around November 1st, Celtic people of ancient Britain held a festival to give thanks for the harvest. Nuts and apples both played an important role, as they represented the fruits being stored for the winter. Both the roasting of nuts and apple bobbing are thought to have originated from this festival.

Pages 14–15  **Today, candy is the best-known Halloween food.** Other foods associated with the holiday include baked goods, such as cookies made in the shape of ghosts or witches. Traditional foods such as nuts, pumpkins, and apples also have connections to Halloween. During Samhain, people often ate special apple cakes called fadge.

Pages 16–17  **Many people decorate their homes for Halloween.** It can be fun to create a scary display using spooky Halloween symbols, such as skeletons or ghosts. Some people visit haunted houses or decorate their own homes to make them appear haunted. Decorations often come in orange and black, since these are the colors traditionally associated with Halloween.

Pages 18–19  **Halloween is a time to help others.** The Trick-or-Treat for UNICEF program was started in 1950. Children all over the United States participate in the program by carrying orange collection boxes on Halloween. While trick-or-treating, they ask for financial donations to UNICEF at each house they visit. The program has raised more than $170 million to help children around the world.

Pages 20–21  **Carving pumpkins into jack-o'-lanterns is a popular Halloween tradition.** Originally, people carved scary faces into their jack-o'-lanterns to scare away evil spirits. They would place a lighted candle inside to make the jack-o'-lantern glow, and leave it in a window. People still light jack-o'-lanterns to show off their carved designs today. For safety reasons, flashlights are sometimes used instead of candles.

KEY WORDS

Research has shown that as much as 65 percent of all written material published in English is made up of 300 words. These 300 words cannot be taught using pictures or learned by sounding them out. They must be recognized by sight. This book contains 54 common sight words to help young readers improve their reading fluency and comprehension. This book also teaches young readers several important content words, such as proper nouns. These words are paired with pictures to aid in learning and improve understanding.

Page	Sight Words First Appearance
4	a, and, as, began, children, day, eat, every, for, in, is, it, of, on, over, the, time, to, up, year
6	by, people, was
7	an, end, means, old, that, word
8	from, go, known, their, well
11	are, often, or, such
12	some
15	food, hand, many, more, other, out
16	homes, used
19	America, help
20	faces, into
21	first, made, were

Page	Content Words First Appearance
4	costumes, Halloween, holiday, October, season, treats
6	Britain, festival, Ireland, Samhain
7	summer
8	activity, candy, neighbors, trick-or-treating
11	choices, monsters, vampires, zombies
12	apples, games, parties
15	chocolate bars, sweets
16	skeletons, spider webs, tombstones
19	money
20	jack-o'-lanterns, pumpkins
21	turnips

Check out www.av2books.com for activities, videos, audio clips, and more!

1. Go to www.av2books.com.
2. Enter book code. G 7 9 3 4 4 4
3. Fuel your imagination online!

www.av2books.com